MUSLIM CHILDREN'S LIBRARY

HILMY THE HIPPO SERIES

HILMY THE HIPPO *Learns to Share*

Author *Rae Norridge*
Illustrator *Leigh Norridge Hodgen*
Designer *Nasir Cadir*
Co-ordinator *Anwar Cara*

Published by
The Islamic Foundation, Markfield Conference Centre
Ratby Lane, Markfield, Leicestershire, LE67 9SY, UK

T (01530) 244 944 F (01530) 244 946
E info@islamic-foundation.org.uk
  publications@islamic-foundation.com

Quran House, PO Box 30611, Nairobi, Kenya

PMB 3193, Kano, Nigeria

British Library Cataloguing in Publication Data

Norridge, Rae
  Hilmy the Hippo learns to share. – (Muslim children's library)
  1. Hilmy the Hippo (Fictitious character) – Juvenile fiction 2. Sharing
  – Juvenile fiction 3. Sharing – Religious aspects – Islam – Juvenile fiction
  4. Children's stories
  I. Title II. Hodgen, Leigh Norridge III. Islamic Foundation (Great Britain)
  823.9'2[J]

ISBN-13: 9780860375852

Printed by Proost International Book Production, Belgium

HILMY THE HIPPO

Rae Norridge

Learns to Share

Illustrated by *Leigh Norridge Hodgen*

THE ISLAMIC FOUNDATION

One bright morning, Hilmy the hippo splashed about in his waterhole. He was in a playful mood. He plunged down beneath the surface of the water and swam to the bottom. Suddenly, and to Hilmy's amazement, he saw three hippos frolicking on the floor of the waterhole.

On seeing Hilmy, the hippos swam to the surface, followed by a very angry Hilmy.

"*As-Salamu 'Alaykum,*" called Hilmy.
"*Wa-'Alaykum as-Salam,*" replied the three hippos.

"What are you doing in my waterhole?" demanded Hilmy.
"You must leave at once. This is my waterhole and I will not
share it with anyone. You must find somewhere else to live."

"Hilmy," said the large hippo. "There has been no rain for
a very long time. Our waterhole has dried up. You must be
kind to us and allow us to share this beautiful waterhole."

3

But Hilmy did not listen, nor did he care.
"Go away!" he shouted. "And don't come back!"
The three hippos sadly left the waterhole.

Later that day a small flock of white-faced ducks flew
down and splashed into the water.

"*As-Salamu 'Alaykum,*" called the ducks.
"*Wa-'Alaykum as-Salam,*" said Hilmy. "Have you come
to share this waterhole too?"

"Of course," replied one of the ducks. "There is very little water about. All the small waterholes have dried up and the river has stopped flowing. It is very sad for everyone. We must pray that it will rain soon."

Hilmy was very annoyed. He angrily shouted at the ducks. "Fly away! Find somewhere else to live. This is my waterhole!"

The white-faced ducks were frightened and flew away.

Day after day the rain did not come. Day after day the waterhole grew smaller and smaller. Soon, the waterhole was nothing but a small pool of dried mud.

Hilmy knew he needed a new place to live, so he set out to find a new waterhole.

He walked a long way across the dry savannah. Soon, he came across a colony of meerkats standing on a mound of sand.

"*As-Salamu 'Alaykum,*" called one of the meerkats.
"*Wa-'Alaykum as-Salam,*" replied Hilmy.
"Where are you heading, Hilmy?" asked the meerkat.

"My waterhole has dried up, so I am looking for a new place to live," replied Hilmy.
"Why are you travelling alone, Hilmy? Have you no friends?"

"I live alone as I do not wish to share," replied Hilmy.

The meerkat looked at Hilmy with surprise. "We live together in large colonies, Hilmy," said the meerkat. "Without each other we would not survive. In times of need, *Insha'Allah* we are there for each other."

"Hmph," snorted Hilmy. "That is not for me."

8

The sun sank low on the horizon and the moon rose
up shining in a bright crescent. Bats swooped across the
night sky and owls hooted from the trees. But Hilmy did
not dally. He continued his search for a new waterhole.

When the sun rose the following day, casting a pink glow across the earth, Hilmy stopped to rest beside the lake. Hundreds and hundreds of flamingos stood feeding in the shallow water.

"*As-Salamu 'Alaykum,*" called Hilmy to the nearest flamingo.

"*Wa-'Alaykum as-Salam,*" replied the beautiful pink bird.

"There are so many of you here," said Hilmy. "How can there be enough food for everyone?"

"We live in large flocks," replied the flamingo. "We always settle where we know there is enough food for everyone. We are gregarious, that is, we like to live together."

Hilmy went on his way, leaving the flamingos to happily feed in the shallow waters of the lake.

Soon, he passed a small herd of zebra. Hilmy noticed that they too, were gregarious. Then he saw a group of giraffes; their heads stood tall above the trees, and Hilmy knew that they too enjoyed each other's company.

By midday, when the sun was directly overhead, Hilmy came to a large sand dune. He raced up the sandy slope, and once at the top, an amazing sight met his eyes. Before him, lay a very large expanse of water. Never before had Hilmy seen so much water. It stretched as far as the horizon.

"Subhanallah!" cried Hilmy. "What a wonderful sight. This is truly the largest waterhole in the world. And there is not a hippo in sight."

Hilmy ran across the white sand and splashed into the water. He had walked for so long that he was very, very thirsty. The first thing he did was to have a large gulp of water.

"*As-Salamu 'Alaykum*," called a seagull
bobbing on the waves.

"*Wa-'Alaykum as-Salam*," replied Hilmy
spitting the water from his mouth. "What is this?" he
spluttered. "This water tastes of salt, I cannot drink this.
I cannot live in this salty water."

"This is the sea, Hilmy, and hippos do not live in
the sea." The seagull explained.

Hilmy turned to leave. He was very disappointed
and he was still very, very thirsty.

15

Hilmy followed the path back to the lake where the flamingos gathered. When he arrived, he went to quench his thirst from the shallow water.

"*As-Salamu 'Alaykum,*" called Hilmy.
"*Wa-'Alaykum as-Salam,*" replied the flamingos. "You cannot drink from our lake, Hilmy," they all chanted. "You must learn a lesson. You would not share your waterhole with others, therefore you cannot drink from our lake. When you are prepared to share, we will share with you. Leave us alone, Hilmy."

16

Hilmy sadly continued on his way. It was a long walk back to his waterhole. The sun beat down and there was no water to be seen.

Once again night fell and Hilmy sat down to rest for a short while. He was still very, very thirsty.

When morning came, Hilmy was eager to be on his way. He passed the little colony of meerkats. They stood on a mound and waved as Hilmy passed by.

Soon, Hilmy passed a small pond where the white-faced ducks had settled. At once Hilmy went over to the water's edge to have a drink.

"Go away, Hilmy!" shouted the white-faced ducks. "You would not share your waterhole with us, therefore you cannot drink our water." With a heavy heart, Hilmy went on his way. He was still very thirsty.

Dark clouds began to gather across the sky and thunder began to rumble in the distance. It began to rain when Hilmy reached another waterhole.

"*As-Salamu 'Alaykum*, Hilmy," called a large hippo.
"Allah in his mercy has sent the rain."

"*Wa-'Alaykum as-Salam*," replied Hilmy.
"Can I share your waterhole?"

"No," called the hippos. "You cannot share our waterhole as you did not allow us to share yours. You must go on your way. Perhaps you will learn that when others are in need you will willingly share your good fortune."

The rain splashed down as Hilmy made his way across the vast savannah.

When Hilmy reached his waterhole he saw his friend, the little chameleon, sitting on a branch. His waterhole was almost full once again.

"As-Salamu 'Alaykum," called the chameleon.
"Wa-'Alaykum as-Salam," replied Hilmy.

"I hope you have learnt your lesson, Hilmy," said the chameleon. "You are fortunate to have such a beautiful waterhole. We must never forget to appreciate the good times, for in life there is always a chance the good times will change. We must help and share with others when they are facing hardships."

Hilmy looked across at the shimmering water and the blue sky above. *Subhanallah*, he was truly blessed. He had the best waterhole in the entire world.

"*Astagfirullah*," he said quietly to himself. He had been unkind to his fellow creatures. Allah in His mercy had blessed him. Hilmy knew that it is not only a duty to share with others, it is a privilege.

GLOSSARY
of Islamic Terms

As-Salamu 'Alaykum
Literally "Peace be upon you", the traditional Muslim greeting, offered when Muslims meet each other.

Wa-'Alaykum as-Salam
"Peace be upon you too", is the reply to the greeting, expressing their mutual love, sincerity and best wishes.

Al-Hamdulillah
Literally "Praise be to Allah". It is used for expressing thanks and gratefulness to Allah. This supplication is also used when one sneezes, in order to thank Allah for having relieved discomfort out of His boundless mercy.

Subhanallah
Literally "Glory be to Allah". It reflects a Muslim's appreciation and amazement at observing any manifestation of Allah's greatness.

Insha' Allah
Literally "If Allah so wishes". Used by Muslims to indicate their decision to do something, provided they get help from Allah. It is recommended that whenever Muslims resolve to do something and make a promise, they should add "Insha' Allah".

Jazak Allah
Literally means: "May Allah Reward you" while thanking someone. A Muslim prays that Allah may reward the benefactor.

Some information about
the Animals and Birds

White-faced Ducks
White-faced ducks are related to swans. Apart from Africa, they are found in South America and Madagascar. They eat water plants.

Savannah
A savannah is a large expanse of flat land covered in grass and low vegetation.

Meerkats
Meerkats are smallish mammals that live in colonies. Sometimes there are as many as 40 in one colony. They eat insects, grubs, small mammals, scorpions and lizards.

Flamingo
Flamingos live in large colonies near water rich in salts. Their long legs are useful for wading in deep water. They eat algae and insects.